X   **That's incredible!**
031.02
THA   4/15   AME

ST. MARY PARISH LIBRARY
FRANKLIN, LOUISIANA

Ripley's Believe It or Not!

Developed and produced by Ripley Publishing Ltd

This edition published and distributed by:

Mason Crest
450 Parkway Drive, Suite D, Broomall, PA 19008
www.masoncrest.com

Copyright © 2013 by Ripley Entertainment Inc. This edition printed in 2014.
All rights reserved. Ripley's, Believe It or Not!, and Ripley's Believe It or Not! are registered trademarks of Ripley Entertainment Inc. No part of this publication may be reproduced in whole or in part, or stored in a retrieval system, or transmitted in any form or by any means, electronic, mechanical, photocopying, recording, or otherwise, without written permission from the publishers. For information regarding permission, write to VP Intellectual Property, Ripley Entertainment Inc., Suite 188, 7576 Kingspointe Parkway, Orlando, Florida, 32819
website: ripleybooks.com

Printed and bound in the United States of America

First printing
9 8 7 6 5 4 3 2 1

Ripley's Believe It or Not!
That's Incredible!
ISBN: 978-1-4222-3145-6 (hardback)
Ripley's Believe It or Not!—Complete 8 Title Series
ISBN: 978-1-4222-3138-8

Cataloging-in-Publication Data is on file with the Library of Congress

PUBLISHER'S NOTE
While every effort has been made to verify the accuracy of the entries in this book, the Publishers cannot be held responsible for any errors contained in the work. They would be glad to receive any information from readers.

WARNING
Some of the stunts and activities in this book are undertaken by experts and should not be attempted by anyone without adequate training and supervision.

Dare To Look

THAT'S INCREDIBLE!

www.MasonCrest.com

THAT'S INCREDIBLE!

Wacky world. Discover this extraordinary collection of eccentric tales. Find out about the 1,185-ft (361.4-m) long hair extension, the dog that looks like a lion, and the lake that is filled with over 20 million jellyfish!

Dutch computer experts Erik de Nijs and Tim Smit designed this pair of jeans with a full-size Bluetooth keyboard integrated into the legs...

JELLYFISH LAKE

▶ Jellyfish Lake on Eil Malk, an island in Palau, is home to over 20 million jellyfish—yet people can swim safely among them because, over time, the strength of their sting has been greatly reduced. Isolated for thousands of years from the Pacific Ocean that surrounds the island, the jellyfish thrive in the landlocked, algae-rich lake with no predators. As a result, they don't need a powerful sting, and their lake has become a huge hit with divers.

AUTO MISSILE ▶ Paul Stender of Indianapolis, Indiana, strapped a cruise missile engine to the roof of a 1967 Chevrolet to create a crazy car that could do 300 mph (480 km/h) and fire out 30-ft (9-m) flames from the rear. The 10,000 bhp engine on his Jet-Impala 67 is the equivalent of ten high-powered Bugatti Veyron sports cars. He has previously built a jet-powered toilet and a jet-powered school bus featured in *Ripley's Believe It or Not! Strikingly True*.

OLD FAITHFUL ▶ Rachel Veitch of Orlando, Florida, drove 567,000 mi (912,500 km) over a 48-year period in the same car. She bought her Mercury Comet Caliente in 1964, and it went on to outlast three marriages and 18 battery changes. The 93-year-old grandmother finally had to give up driving it in March 2012 because she had been declared legally blind.

TIGHT SQUEEZE ▶ In Beijing on May 21, 2012, Chinese stunt driver Han Yue parallel-parked his Mini in a space just 6 in (15 cm) longer than his car—in less than two seconds!

GHOST TRAINS ▶ A group of U.K. rail enthusiasts ride on special "Parliamentary trains"—or "ghost trains"—services that are often otherwise empty, and are run just once a week and only in one direction. Train operators run these ghost trains to keep small routes open because it is cheaper and less time-consuming than closing them down.

COLD COMFORT ▶ The NS *Yamal*, a Russian icebreaker ship, will never sail out of the Arctic Sea because its design means it requires the cold waters to cool the two nuclear reactors that power it.

BIGGEST FLOTILLA ▶ Queen Elizabeth II helped set a new world record for the largest parade of boats after leading a 1,000-strong flotilla along London's River Thames on June 3, 2012, as part of her Diamond Jubilee celebrations.

SWEET RIDE ▶ Fritz Grobe and Stephen Voltz of Buckfield, Maine, built a single-seat rocket car powered only by soda and candy. They used the chemical reaction—a process called nucleation—that occurs as a result of mixing 54 bottles of fizzy Coke Zero and 324 Mentos to propel the car a distance of 239 ft (73 m).

BRIDGE FIRE

▶ The 100-car Union Pacific coal train was traveling from Denver, Colorado, to Chicago, Illinois, when a wheel bearing on the train overheated and melted, causing white hot molten metal to fall down onto the rail. Spotting the smoke coming from the 57th car, the alert crew immediately stopped the train but unfortunately the hot wheel was directly over Turkey Creek Bridge near Sharon Springs, Kansas. As the wooden structure caught fire, the crew saved the rest of the train by unhooking it from the cars that were stopped on the bridge, but the accident still caused $2 million damage.

THAT'S INCREDIBLE!

HEAVY PENALTY ▶ In January 2012, railroad officials in Indonesia began suspending weighted balls over railroad tracks to discourage "train surfing"—the practice of commuters riding on train roofs without paying a fare.

POOP POWER ▶ On March 22, 2012, the Denver Zoo in Colorado demonstrated a three-wheeled motorized rickshaw—or tuk tuk—that runs on a mixture of trash generated by zoo visitors and employees, and animal poop.

DESERT REPAIRS ▶ When Frenchman Emile Leray crashed his Citroën 2CV car into a rock in the middle of the Moroccan desert, leaving it undrivable, he reached the safety of a village some 20 mi (32 km) away by building a makeshift motorbike out of the wrecked car. Using the limited tools he had with him, the 43-year-old retired electrician began by removing the Citroën's body, which he then used as a shelter for sleep. To build the bike, he shortened the car's chassis before reattaching the axles and two of the wheels, as well as installing the engine and gearbox in the middle. After 12 days, by which time he had just one pint of water left, he was ready to ride off to the village, but even then he kept falling off the bike's seat, which was made from part of the car's rear bumper.

SUBWAY SYSTEM ▶ New York City has a land area of 302.6 sq mi (784 sq km)—but its subway system has 842 mi (1,355 km) of track.

FRENCH LESSON ▶ A confused driver drove down the steps of a Paris Metro station after mistaking it for an underground parking lot. He managed to brake in time to stop the car on the steps of the Chaussée d'Antin-La Fayette station but left the back wheels sticking out on the sidewalk.

FISHY PASSENGER
▶ This successful fisherman in Jinja, Uganda, decided there was only one way to take his monster catch home—on the back of his motorcycle.

BAD IDEA ▶ A drunk driver caused a railway in Wuhan, China, to be closed for five hours when he tried to drive home along the tracks. The man told police he didn't know the area and blamed his "misleading" GPS system. He made it about 100 yards when the metal rails shredded his tires and his car became stuck. Luckily, he was spotted before passenger trains started moving the following morning.

ROCKET MAN ▶ In June 2012, daredevil Swiss rocket man Yves Rossy dropped from a helicopter and deployed his four-engined Jetwing flying suit alongside a vintage Breitling passenger plane at an altitude of 4,500 ft (1,370 m) over Lake Lucerne, Switzerland. He flew for seven minutes at 128 mph (205 km/h) until his fuel ran out and he parachuted safely to the ground.

CHIPPED BODYWORK ▶ Zhang Lianzhi of Tianjin, China, has covered a brand new Range Rover in 10,000 pieces of broken antique porcelain. He spent nearly 20 years collecting porcelain chips from all corners of China before sticking them to the vehicle. Even though they are broken, the bits of ceramic are worth an estimated $157,000.

▲ This is the moment when the wooden railroad bridge burst into flames and collapsed in a freak accident that sent six 280,000-lb (127,000-kg) train cars crashing into the creek below.

BONE IDOL

▶ Biker Phil Boxall has ridden more than 32,000 mi (51,000 km) around the U.K. on his 1200cc Yamaha V-Max with a human skeleton as his passenger! Bought on eBay, "Sid Bones" has ridden everywhere with Phil for more than four years. The pair even once reached a bone-rattling 120 mph (193 km/h) in just 12 seconds on a drag strip.

SNAKES ALIVE!
▶ A Brazilian motorcyclist doing 164 mph (262 km/h) on an open road had the shock of his life when a yellow snake suddenly lunged at him from near the right handlebar and came to rest on his hand. Luckily, the biker kept his cool and pulled over to the side of the road. The snake had probably been hiding in the bike's engine to keep warm.

THAT'S INCREDIBLE!

MILKING

▶ Students from Newcastle upon Tyne, England, pour 4-pint (2-l) containers of milk over their heads in public as part of an Internet craze called "milking," a new rival to "planking." A YouTube video, created by 22-year-old Tom Morris, quickly went viral with its clips of students drenching themselves in milk in shopping malls, in the middle of busy traffic islands, outside bars, and even up a tree.

COMPUTER WEDDING ▶ When web designer Miguel Hanson married Diana Wesley in July 2011 in Houston, Texas, the wedding ceremony was conducted by a computer. Unable to get a friend to officiate, the groom programmed a computer to perform the role instead, creating on a 30-in (75-cm) monitor the face of a virtual minister, Rev. Bit, who recited instructions such as "You may kiss the bride" in a robotic voice.

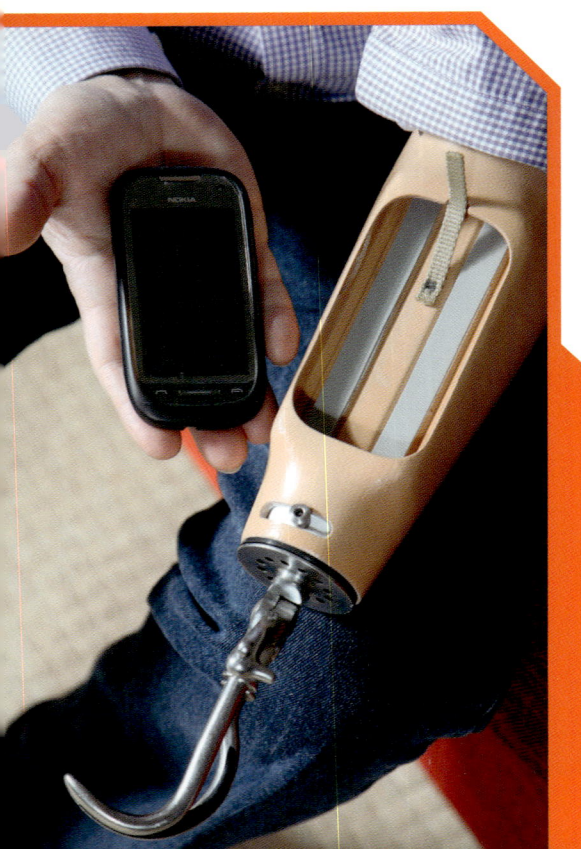

SMART ARM
▶ Trevor Prideaux from Somerset, England, became the first person to have a smartphone built into his prosthetic arm. Born without a left arm, he used to have to balance his phone on the false arm or on a flat surface to use it, but now that a Nokia C7 has been embedded into the fiberglass and laminate limb, he simply calls and texts using his right hand.

WRONG BOX ▶ After ordering a 39-in flat-screen TV from Amazon, Seth Horvitz opened the parcel at his Washington, D.C., home and found that it contained a high-powered, military-grade assault rifle instead of his TV.

VIDEO CHARACTERS ▶ In New Berlin, Wisconsin, in 2011, 425 people dressed as characters from video games including Angry Birds, Super Mario Bros, Halo 3 and Pac-Man.

VIRTUAL BRIDESMAID ▶ Stranded 1,600 mi (2,575 km) away in Virginia, Renee Armstrong still managed to take part in the wedding of her best friend Jamie Wilborn by following her down the aisle in Denver, Colorado, on an iPad. An usher carried a white iPad connected to Armstrong's webcam and the absent bridesmaid even made it into the wedding photos.

SOCCER TWEET ▶ Fernando Torres' last-minute goal for Chelsea in the Champions League semi-final second leg against Barcelona on April 24, 2012, attracted 13,684 tweets per second, breaking the sports tweets record of 12,233 during the climax of the 2012 Super Bowl between the New York Giants and New England Patriots.

MAGIC POTIONS ▶ Online auction site eBay banned the sale of potions and spells in 2012 after buyers kept complaining that the products failed to bring them instant wealth or make them stunningly beautiful.

TWISTED VISION ▶ Lithuanian photographer Tadas Cerniauskas invited 100 people to his studio in Vilnius to have their faces blasted with a high-powered jet of air from an industrial leaf blower so that he could capture the effect it had on their mouth, eyes, and hair. When posted on his Facebook page, the pictures got three million views in just a week.

WI-FI DONKEYS ▶ Kfar Kedem, an Israeli tourist attraction dedicated to showing how people lived in Old Testament times, fitted its donkeys with Wi-Fi routers so that visitors dressed in biblical robes and headdresses could have Internet access at all times.

▶ **THE AVERAGE CELL PHONE CONTAINS AT LEAST 18 TIMES MORE BACTERIA THAN A TOILET SEAT.** ◀

BADLY STUFFED ▶ A Facebook page dedicated to bizarre or incompetent taxidermy has attracted some 13,000 likes. "Badly Stuffed Animals" includes such strange items as a dead dog riding a tricycle, a camel in a suitcase, and a dog leap-frogging a globe.

TIME-LAPSE TRIP ▶ Photographer Brian Defrees from Syracuse, New York State, made a time-lapse video of his 12,225-mi (19,560-km) trip around the United States and posted the result on YouTube in a five-minute film that he made from more than 200,000 individual photos. Mounting a camera on his car, he set it to take a picture every five seconds as he crossed more than 30 states in 55 days.

HOMER BLOB ▶ While cleaning out a cupboard, Christopher Herbert from London, England, discovered a blob of dried glue that his girlfriend said resembled Homer Simpson—and when he put it up for sale on eBay, it sold for a staggering £152,200 ($236,000) after attracting 85 bids.

MISTAKEN IDENTITY ▶ At the height of the 2010–11 Ashes cricket series between England and Australia, Ashley Kerekes of Westfield, Massachusetts, received dozens of unwanted tweets simply because her Twitter account was named @theashes. When she protested that she was not a cricket match, her follower count jumped from 300 to 13,500 and she was offered a free trip to Australia.

IRAN BAN ▶ Protests by young gamers in Iran persuaded the country's government to ban the bestselling U.S. video game Battlefield 3, which depicts American soldiers invading Iran in search of missing nuclear warheads in 2014.

MONEY FACING ▶ There are Facebook groups dedicated to an Internet craze called "Money Facing" in which people have their photo taken with a folded banknote in front of their face. Hundreds of people have created facial hybrids of themselves with the likes of Queen Elizabeth II and Charles Darwin by posing with banknotes from all over the world.

FISHY BUSINESS

▶ Nearly 10,000 people used a website's online tool to design colorful sneakers that, it was claimed, would be grown to order by mixing and matching stingray DNA—unaware that the whole enterprise was an elaborate hoax. Advertised as a Thai company, Rayfish Footwear attracted widespread media coverage but was actually created by a team of Dutch designers. Far from being genetically modified, the beautifully patterned shoes were dyed with simple paint.

HELPING HAND ▶ A giant green hand protruding from a large manhole in the road startled drivers in Tianjin, China. With the manhole missing its cover for more than a month, local residents stuffed an abandoned hand-shaped sofa down it to warn motorists of the hazard ahead.

CRAZY BIKE ▶ Zhang Yali from Jilin City, China, built a larger-than-life bike—more than 10 ft (3 m) high and 18 ft (5.5 m) long—for his cartoon-crazy son. It cost him $3,000 to create the one-ton bike, which has two huge wheels taken from an excavator. The seat is made from old sofas, and can sit up to eight people in two rows.

SCHOOLBOY HERO ▶ When the driver of his school bus suffered a heart attack on the morning of April 9, 2012, quick-thinking 13-year-old Jeremy Wuitschick of Milton, Washington State, grabbed the steering wheel, directed the bus safely toward a curb, and pulled the key from the ignition. He then began performing chest compressions on the unconscious driver.

ALTERNATIVE HEATER ▶ When the heater in his Volvo broke, Pascal Prokop of Mettmenstetten, Switzerland, overcame the bitter cold of the Swiss winter by installing a functional wood-burning stove in the car. He removed the passenger seat in order to accommodate the stove and also installed a chimney to get rid of the carbon monoxide and smoke. Swiss officials had no objection to his unconventional modifications.

LONG RIDE ▶ Paul Archer, Johno Ellison, and Leigh Purnell from the U.K. traveled a mind-boggling 43,320 mi (69,716 km) on a 15-month journey around the world in a black London taxi cab. They racked up almost $120,000 on the meter during a trip that took them to four continents and 50 different countries. They were arrested in Moscow and were nearly kidnapped in Pakistan, but also achieved the highest taxi ride ever when they drove up to the Mount Everest base camp, which lies 17,143 ft (5,225 m) above sea level.

MASS BURNOUT

THAT'S INCREDIBLE!

SCRAP BATPOD Batman fan Vu Tung Lam from Lang Son, Vietnam, built his own version of the Caped Crusader's motorbike, the Batpod, from scrap metal and an old Suzuki engine. It took him two months and $450 to build, but although the machine has a top speed of 56 mph (90 km/h), he is not permitted to ride it on Vietnamese roads.

SPEED SLIDE A Swiss motorcyclist set off a police speed camera, while sliding along the ground having fallen off his bike. After losing control of his machine, Boris Maier from Bern, was clocked hurtling helplessly at 67 mph (108 km/h) in a 50-mph (80-km/h) zone while the riderless bike's speed went unrecorded.

FARE POINT For a $5,000 fare, New York City cab driver Mohammed Alam took John Belitsky and Dan Wuebben on a six-day, 2,800-mi (4,500-km) drive to Los Angeles, California—with a stopover in Las Vegas, Nevada, for a night of gambling where they won $2,000. A first-class return air fare was just under $4,000, but Belitsky wanted to prove that his father, a former New York City cab driver, was wrong when he said no cabbie would take them all the way to L.A.

ROAD LEGAL Engineer Russ Bost from Essex, England, has created a road-legal Formula-1 look-alike car out of spare parts. His custom-built machine has a motorcycle engine and a top speed of 170 mph (274 km/h). It only costs $15,000 to buy and does 30 miles per gallon (10.6 km/liter), compared to an F1 car's measly 3.8 miles per gallon (1.3 km/liter). It also has a rear seat for carrying groceries back from the supermarket in style.

LUXURY HEARSE Italian custom builder Biemme Special Cars created a $600,000, 23-ft-long (7-m), stretch hearse, made entirely from aluminum and constructed from more than 600 assembled parts and 660 ft (200 m) of welding. The coffin compartment of the Rolls-Royce Phantom Hearse B12 features high luminescence LEDs to illuminate the casket.

FLYING SAUCER Intrepid farmer Shu Mansheng successfully flew his homemade flying saucer at an altitude of 6 ft (1.8 m) or more for over 30 seconds in Wuhan, China. He spent $4,500 building the 18-ft-diameter (5.5-m) octocopter, which is powered by eight motorbike engines with propellers.

OLDEST BACKPACKER Keith Wright from Queensland, Australia, loves traveling around the world with his backpack—even though he is 95 years old. He took up backpacking when he was 85, and has visited more than 20 countries and 100 foreign cities.

SPEED SAIL A sailing boat traveled at an astonishing speed of 43.2 mph (69.5 km/h) over one nautical mile in San Francisco Bay on August 31, 2012. Designed by French yachtsman Alain Thébault, L' Hydroptère rises up out of the water on hydrofoils as it picks up speed.

TWO-WHEEL DRIVE British stunt driver Terry Grant drove a Nissan Juke car over a 1-mile (1.6-km) course at the 2011 Goodwood Festival of Speed in an amazing 2 minutes 55 seconds—driving sideways on only two wheels. His average speed was just over 20 mph (32 km/h).

BEE SWARM A flight from Pittsburgh, Pennsylvania, to New York City was delayed at Pittsburgh International Airport on August 1, 2012, after a swarm of thousands of honeybees suddenly gathered on the airplane's wing.

DOZED OFF Patrice Christine Ahmed, a French woman flying from Pakistan to Paris, slept through the landing at Charles de Gaulle Airport and didn't wake up until she was on the way back to Lahore!

FREE TRAVEL After running away from his mother during a shopping trip, 11-year-old Liam Corcoran-Fort was able to fly from Manchester, England, to Rome, Italy, despite not having a ticket, a boarding pass, or a passport.

HOMEMADE PLANE Retired pilot Patrick Elliott and his wife Linda, from Surrey, England, circumnavigated the globe in a tiny homemade airplane, which they had spent 16 years building. The couple took off around the world in the 16-ft-long (5-m) Rutan Long-EZ in September 2010, flying a total of 37,398 mi (60,186 km) before returning home a year and a day later. In the course of their epic journey, they made 99 flights, visited 23 countries, and used $18,000-worth of fuel.

FAKE FERRARI The Fahrradi Farfalla FFX looks like a new Ferrari, but it is actually a quad-cycle with a top speed barely any faster than that of a pedestrian. Created by Austrian artist Hannes Langeder using plastic and lightweight steel, the unique cycle, based on the exterior of a Ferrari FXX, weighs just 220 lb (100 kg) and is steered using pedals that control 11 different gears.

▶ At Australia's biggest horsepower party, the Summernats 26 festival in Canberra, 69 cars revved up furiously for 30 seconds, creating billowing clouds of red and white smoke and black rubber to set a new world record for the largest simultaneous burnout.

NEAR MISSES

BALANCING ACT

▼ Shan Dan avoided disaster by a matter of inches after mistaking the gas pedal for the brake while reverse parking and leaving her BMW hanging precariously over the edge of an elevated parking garage in Changchun, China. She calmly climbed out but said: "I was terrified when I got out and saw the position of the car."

AMAZING ESCAPE

▼ Driver Yang Junsheng incredibly escaped with barely a scratch after dozens of steel bars crashed through the windshield of his car in Taizhou, China. He smashed into the back of a pickup truck carrying the metal rods but instinctively ducked as they flew toward him, and somehow they all missed him.

NEAR MISS

▲ A driver in Zhenjiang, China, had a lucky escape after he drove into a metal road barrier, which speared through the front of his van and straight out of the back, missing him by inches. He suffered nothing worse than a scratch on his left leg, but passed out due to shock.

CAR WRECKER

▲ Alex Habay was sitting in his car at a traffic light in Meadville, Pennsylvania, when a 1,500-lb (680-kg) wrecking ball suddenly smashed into the rear with such force that it pushed his vehicle into the two cars in front of him. The runaway ball had broken loose from a demolition crane and careened down the street, hitting nine parked cars before crashing into Habay's trunk where the presence of eight soccer balls may have lessened the impact and saved him from serious injury.

CLIFF HANGER

◀ This BMW car finished up just a few feet from the edge of a steep cliff and a 100-ft (30-m) drop to the sea below after hurtling down a grassy bank at Flamborough Head in Yorkshire, England. The driver was winched to safety by rescue helicopter.

CRAZY CROSSING

▶ This car driver had an unbelievable escape after sneaking over a level crossing in Carmarthenshire, Wales, just a split second ahead of an oncoming train. The driver, who had his wife and young son in the car at the time, later admitted dangerous driving. He said he had not seen the flashing warning lights at the crossing.

SMART FEEDER ▶ Pet owners can now feed their animals remotely—using a smartphone. Carlos Herrera from Los Angeles, California, has invented the Pintofeed, an automated feeder that connects to an app enabling owners to hit the feed button on their phone from anywhere in the world to ensure their pet never misses a meal. The feeder even tweets owners afterward to let them know how much the animal has eaten.

CAT APPEAL ▶ A U.S. company has developed a series of iPad apps for cats. Little Hiccup's first app features a fast-moving virtual mouse to appeal to cats' hunting instincts as they try to catch it, and it proved so successful that a sequel was launched called "Paint For Cats," where the cat makes a colorful paw imprint every time it touches the screen.

BALANCING DOG ▶ Nick Johnson of Norfolk, England, spent up to five hours a day teaching Ozzy, his chocolate Border collie-kelpie cross, to balance on all four paws on a thin metal chain attached to two posts and then to stand on his hind legs without falling off. Filmed by a stunned passerby on his cell phone, the footage was uploaded to YouTube, where it attracted more than 80,000 hits on its first day.

PRIEST'S CONFESSION ▶ Father Massimo Donghi, a priest from Besana in Brianza, Italy, had to explain to parishioners how he came to be rescued from the wreck of luxury cruise ship *Costa Concordia* in January 2012 after originally telling them he was taking time off to spend a couple of weeks at a spiritual retreat. His deception was uncovered when his niece Elisabetta, who was with him on the cruise, posted on Facebook that she and all her family "including Uncle Massimo" were safe.

RECORD GAME ▶ In an event that took place simultaneously in New York and London on June 26, 2012, Kathleen Henkel of Oakland, New Jersey, and Laura Rich of Cardiff, Wales, both played the video card game Solitaire Blitz on Facebook for a record 30 hours straight, in total playing more than 1,500 hands.

MANY MONSTERS ▶ In March 2012, U.S. pop star Lady Gaga became the first person to rack up 20 million Twitter followers. She calls her fans "little monsters."

TALKING TO HIMSELF ▶ Filmmaker Jeremiah McDonald of Portland, Maine, produced a YouTube video—20 years in the making—in which he interviewed his 12-year-old self. Editing together interview footage of himself at age 12 and, in 2012, at age 32, he makes it appear as if he is talking to his child self about a range of subjects including *Star Wars*, *Doctor Who*, and dead pets.

STOLEN CAR ▶ In 2012—42 years after it had been stolen—Bob Russell of Dallas, Texas, tracked down his 1967 Austin Healey in Los Angeles, California, when the car was put up for sale on eBay.

TRUE BELIEBERS ▶ Canadian pop star Justin Bieber's charity rallying call on his 18th birthday on March 1, 2012, attracted a world record 322,224 tweets and re-tweets from his fans.

DIGITALLY ALTERED

▶ *An artist from Bologna, Italy, using the pseudonym Dito Von Tease ("dito" is Italian for "finger") converts the tip of his index finger into famous faces by creating different skin colors and features and adding hairstyles and makeup. Each face takes him up to 16 hours to make, and his portfolio includes such diverse characters as* **Star Trek**'s **Mr. Spock, a Kayan woman with a brass-ringed neck, Steve Jobs, Sherlock Holmes, the Dalai Lama, and Mickey Mouse.** *He had the idea when looking for an original avatar for his profile picture on Facebook, and he chose a finger portrait in order to conceal his identity.*

Mr. Spock

Kayan woman

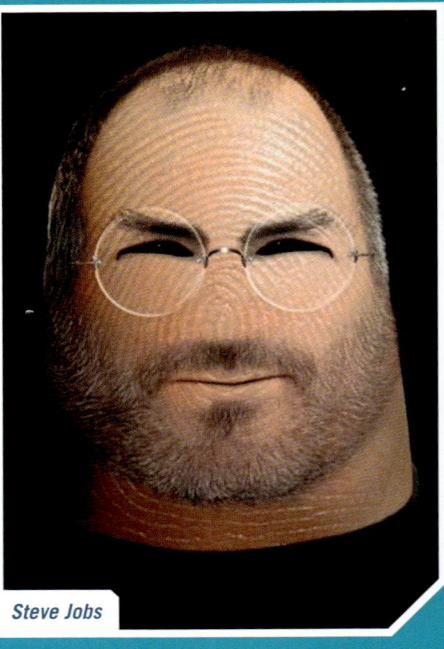
Steve Jobs

SHELL SHOCK

▶ Maia, a grieving chicken owned by Ashley Wood of Somerset, England, was coaxed into laying eggs again by watching videos of other birds on an iPad. She had stopped producing eggs after her companion chicken, Baba, was eaten by a fox, but with the help of the iPad she was soon laying five a week.

THAT'S INCREDIBLE!

NEW SPIN▶ Design student and games enthusiast Lee Wei Chen from London, England, combined a washing machine with a video game console, the progress of the washing cycle being dependent on the success of the person playing the game.

STATUS UPDATE▶ When Facebook founder Mark Zuckerberg got married to longtime girlfriend Priscilla Chan in a surprise ceremony on May 19, 2012, his status update on his Facebook Timeline received 1,045,272 likes, appropriately setting a new record for most likes on a Facebook item.

RECYCLED TREE HOUSE▶ Joel Allen built an egg-shaped tree house in the woods near Whistler, Canada, from thousands of dollars of recycled materials donated through Craigslist over several months.

TEEN EXCELS▶ Fifteen-year-old Rebecca Rickwood of Cambridgeshire, England, beat 228,000 international rivals to be crowned the world champion user of Microsoft's Excel 2007 spreadsheet software in a timed contest in San Diego, California.

WEDDING INVASION▶ Bride Lee Su and groom Ming found what they thought was a quiet woodland clearing in Nanjing, China, for their romantic wedding photos—but seconds later it was invaded by hundreds of computer game fans playing a real-life reconstruction of *Counter Strike*.

TECHNO CAT▶ A cat named Tiger Lily regularly plays with her owner's iPad for up to 15 minutes at a time. The cat is so fascinated by the technology that Anne Druais of Sydney, Australia, has to keep a plastic screen guard over the iPad to protect it from Tiger Lily's claws.

▶ **MORE PEOPLE ON THE PLANET OWN A CELL PHONE THAN A TOOTHBRUSH.** ◀

WRONG MAP▶ A group of schoolchildren from Normandy, France, who were on an exchange trip to the town of Ipswich in Suffolk, England, were hopelessly lost until they were told by a local tourist information office that the maps they had downloaded from the Internet were of Ipswich, Queensland, Australia, 10,000 mi (16,000 km) away.

FACEBOOK RESCUE▶ Waking up paralyzed and with the battery in his cell phone dead, Peter Casaru of Brecon, Wales, received quick medical treatment thanks to his friends on Facebook. He managed to crawl to his laptop and post that he was unable to move his legs or call for an ambulance. Friends from as far away as New York and Vancouver offered to help, but it was Juliet McFarlane from 6 mi (9.6 km) away who was first to call an ambulance.

LAPTOP COMPUTER
▶ Dutch computer experts Erik de Nijs and Tim Smit have designed a pair of jeans with a full-size Bluetooth keyboard integrated into the upper leg. The $375 jeans, which give the wearer freedom of movement around a room while still being in control of the computer, operate via a USB device plugged into the computer port and also feature speakers and a wireless mouse.

FACE SPOOK

▶ In June 2012, Ripley's employee Charlotte Howell of Essex, England, took a seemingly uneventful photograph at Highgate Cemetery in North London. When she uploaded the image to Facebook, the automatic recognition software picked out something nobody had noticed: a ghostly face among the headstones, which the site tried to tag as a real person. Charlotte testifies that nobody else was in the area when the photo was taken.

WALKING WEBSITE ▶ Patrick Vaillancourt from Montreal, Canada, has more than 15,000 Internet addresses tattooed all over his body. With profits going to charity, he charges sites $35 to have their URL permanently inked into his skin, the price rising to $500 for prime positions and large tattoos. He hopes eventually to have 100,000 URL tattoos on his body, which would take at least 10,000 hours of inking to create.

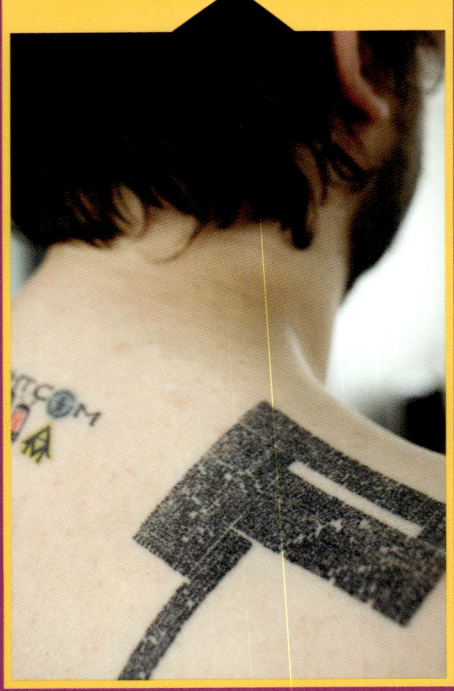

BANK CRISIS ▶ When British bank NatWest suffered a major computer glitch in June 2012, hundreds of Twitter users voiced their frustration to @Natwest, unaware that it was the Twitter account name chosen by Natalie Westerman, a 22-year-old schoolteacher from Newcastle upon Tyne.

PIANO BOY ▶ Ethan Walmark, a six-year-old autistic boy from Westport, Connecticut, became an Internet sensation with his YouTube version of Billy Joel's "Piano Man," racking up 640,000 hits in just five days. He learned to play the piano at age four—by ear.

CUTTING EDGE ▶ A video of an Ecuadorian man using a piranha as a pair of scissors went viral on YouTube. Taken in the Cuyabeno Rainforest, the clip shows the fish, held tightly in the man's hand, using its razor-sharp teeth to slice instantly through a twig placed in its open jaws.

ANGRY BRIDES ▶ Inspired by the popular Angry Birds game, a new Indian online game called Angry Brides seeks to highlight the practice of illegal dowry demands in India. In Angry Brides, players attack prospective dowry-hungry grooms—an engineer, a doctor, and a pilot—with a variety of weapons, including a brick-red stiletto shoe and a broomstick.

VIRTUALLY MARRIED ▶ On Valentine's Day 2012, 21,879 marriages took place in the online role-playing game Rift, setting a record for the most in-game marriages in 24 hours.

BEYOND THE GRAVE ▶ An Israeli-produced app, "If I Die," allows people to compose their final Facebook update, which is then posted after their death. Three Facebook friends are nominated as trustees to guard the posthumous text or video message before hitting the publish button once the person has died.

POPULAR POST ▶ Led by Tracey Hodgson of the U.K. and Cathy Matthews of Sacramento, California, 107 people—mostly fans of the game FrontierVille—joined forces and posted a record 1,001,598 comments on a single Facebook item. Each person commented on the original post an average of about 9,350 times.

FATAL FRIEND ▶ After defrauding banks in Seattle, Washington State, Maxi Sopo fled to Mexico where he boasted about his freedom on Facebook. Then he made the mistake of adding a former Justice Department official to his list of friends, a move that landed him in a Mexican jail and led to his extradition back to the United States where he was eventually sentenced to 33 months in prison.

DARING JUMP ▶ A YouTube video captures the moment a daredevil young Russian BASE jumper had a miraculous escape when his parachute failed to open after he had jumped from a 400-ft-high (120-m) pylon. Although snow cushioned his fall, he still suffered fractured vertebrae, pelvis, and legs and could not walk again for three months.

ROBBERY FOILED ▶ A man from Essex, England, foiled a raid on his home by shouting at burglars via a webcam from Turkey 1,500 mi (2,400 km) away. The man, who was attending a funeral abroad, was talking to his family back home in England via Skype when he spotted two strangers in the hallway after his wife had briefly left the room. He yelled at them to get out of his house and they fled empty-handed.

VIDEO GLASSES ▶ Skydivers jumped from a blimp above San Francisco wearing new Google glasses that video everything they see—and a live camera feed from the glasses meant that people on the ground were able to watch footage of the jump from the skydivers' perspective.

APE PADS ▶ Orangutans at Jungle Island Zoo in Miami, Florida, are being encouraged to use iPads in the hope that they will eventually be able to communicate with keepers and visitors. The younger apes, in particular, have taken to the handheld computer tablets, and enjoy drawing and playing games on them.

GOOGLE HUNT ▶ An Indian boy who became separated from his mother in 1986 found her 25 years later from his new home in Tasmania, Australia, after using Google Earth to trace her. Saroo Brierley was five when he got lost on a 14-hour train journey. He ended up in Calcutta, where he was taken in by an orphanage and eventually adopted by a couple from Tasmania. Years later, through satellite computer images, he managed to identify his Indian hometown of Khandwa and when he traveled there he was reunited with his birth mother.

PHONE INTERRUPTION ▶ After a member of the audience forgot to switch off a cell phone during a solo classical music concert, interrupting the concert with a distinctive ringtone, Slovakian violinist Lukas Kmit took his opportunity to highlight the unfortunate incident by pausing for a moment and then continuing his performance with an improvised version of the ringtone.

STREET LIFE
▶ Google Street View has thrown up some bizarre images in Tokyo, Japan, including a seemingly headless pedestrian walking down the street toward a burst of white light.

GAMING LIZARD ▶ Crunch, a bearded dragon lizard owned by Philip Gith of Brisbane, Australia, uses her tongue to "eat" on-screen insects in the Ant Smasher game on Gith's smartphone. She is so fast that a clip of her gaming soon attracted more than six million views on YouTube.

PHONE COSTUMES ▶ To raise money for charity, 330 people dressed up as cell phones at Caterham School in Surrey, England, in July 2012.

LIFE SALE ▶ So that he could start a new life, weathy businessman Shane Butcher from Tampa Bay, Florida, put his old life up for sale on eBay for $3.5 million. He sold off his chain of computer game shops, two waterfront homes, three cars, and even his pet dog.

TWEET LIFE ▶ Just 0.5 percent of Twitter's total population attracts nearly 50 percent of all attention on the microblogging site. In fact, a quarter of Twitter users have no followers at all. Of the 400-million tweets that are sent every day, more than 70 percent gain no response, and 40 percent of Twitter users never tweet at all.

COMPUTER KID ▶ Born in 2006, Wasik Farhan-Roopkotha of Bangladesh began to master complex video games aged just two, and knew how to program and download games at the tender age of four. Wasik says he now has ambitions to be a computer expert and to work for a large computer company in the future.

MOO-SIVE COW

▶ This brown swiss cow is huge! The nine-year-old measures 75 in (190 cm) tall and lives on Jo-Dee Swiss farm in Oregon with owner Jodi Coppini and her family.

THAT'S INCREDIBLE!

BIRD TWEETS ▶ British ornithologist and broadcaster Bill Oddie translated the different calls of tropical birds at the London Zoo and tweeted each interpretation out on Twitter in a maximum 140 characters.

SACRED COMPUTERS ▶ In January 2012, the Swedish government formally recognized the Church of Kopimism, a religious group that promotes distribution of knowledge and claims that computer file sharing ("kopyacting") is a sacred act.

DOOR CLIMBER ▶ "Spider-Girl" Sofya Dickson, age 3, from Leicestershire, England, can climb a 6-ft (1.8-m) doorframe—several times her own height. Her dad Peter only uploaded the video of her acrobatics to YouTube so that her aunt could see it, but it became a worldwide Internet hit and led to requests from American TV shows.

ROCKING CHARGER ▶ A Swiss company has invented the iRock, a rocking chair that charges iPads and iPhones. The $1,700-wooden chair generates enough power from its rocking motion to recharge an iPad 3 to 35 percent in an hour.

LAURA UNSAFE ▶ Laura Safe, a newsreader on the Capital FM Breakfast Show, was so engrossed in texting her boyfriend that she walked straight into a freezing canal in Birmingham, England. She was rescued from the icy water by a passerby, but not before the drama had been captured on CCTV, ensuring that on this occasion she made the news!

MARCHING GAMES ▶ During the half-time break at a university football match against Nebraska in June 2012, a total of 225 members of the Ohio State University Marching Band recreated images from Space Invaders, Pokemon, Tetris, Halo, The Legend of Zelda, and other classic video games.

DONALD DUCK ▶ A lawyer in Zadar, Croatia, complained that Judge Domagoj Kurobasa was not serious-minded enough to try an important libel case because the judge used a picture of Donald Duck for his Facebook profile.

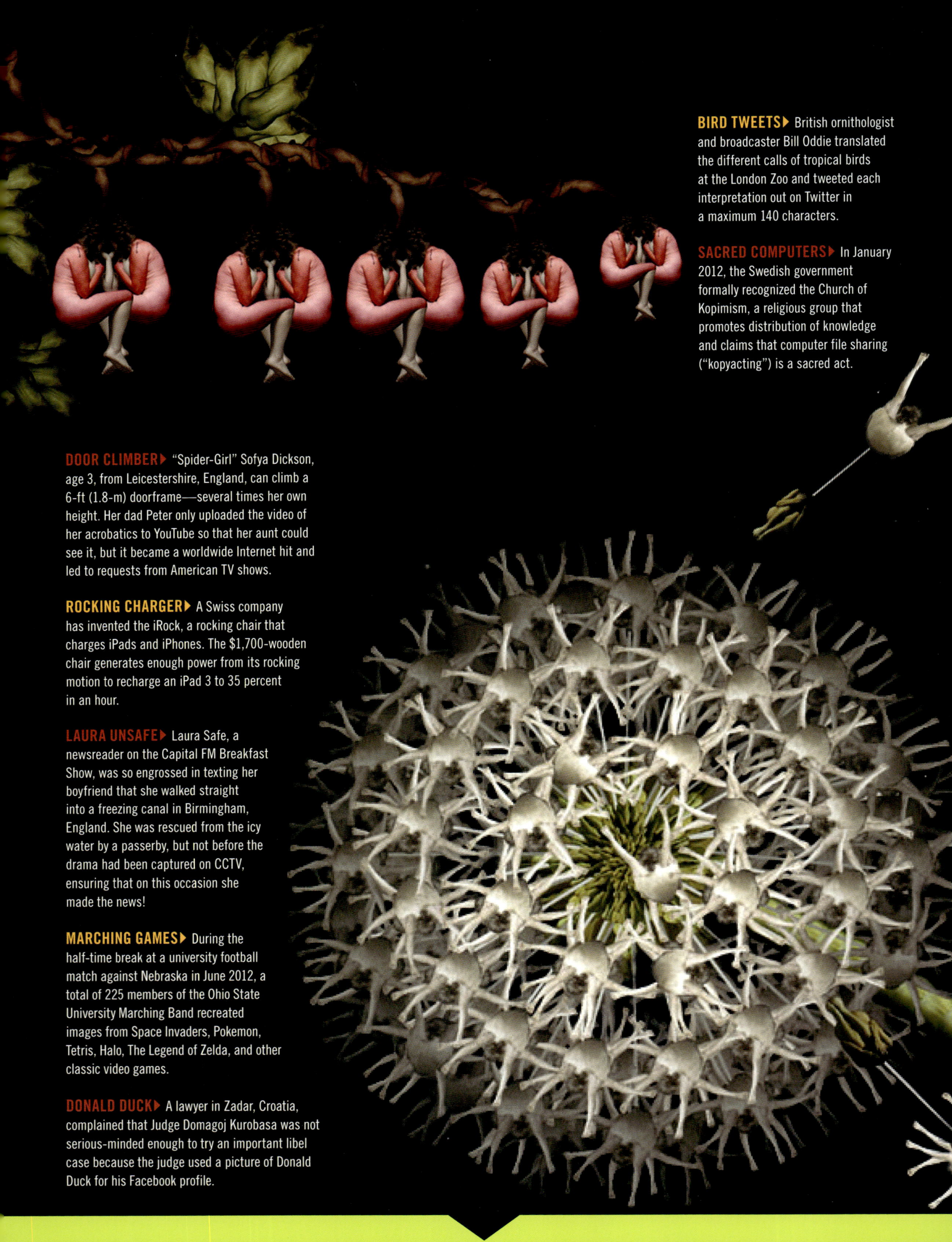

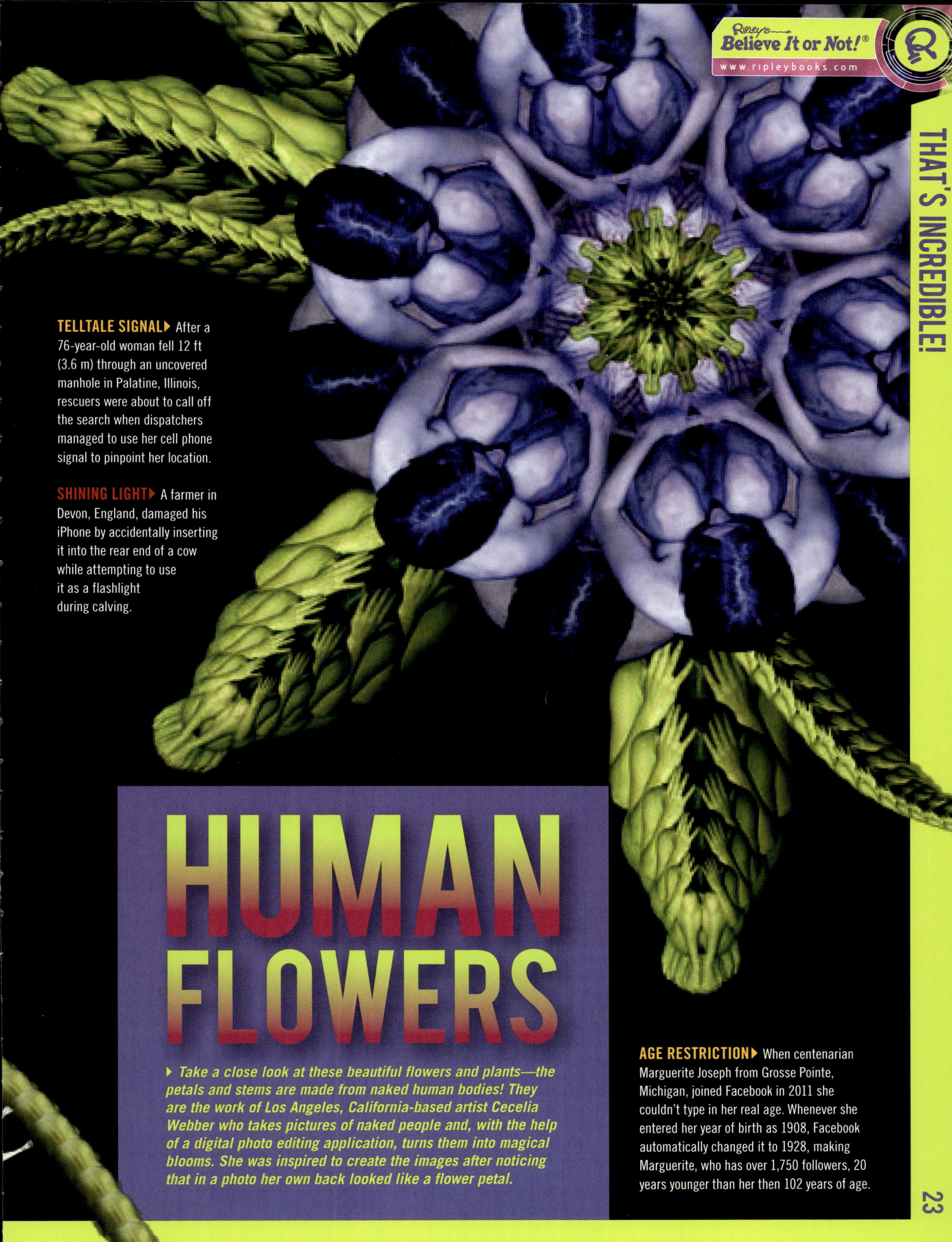

THAT'S INCREDIBLE!

TELLTALE SIGNAL ▶ After a 76-year-old woman fell 12 ft (3.6 m) through an uncovered manhole in Palatine, Illinois, rescuers were about to call off the search when dispatchers managed to use her cell phone signal to pinpoint her location.

SHINING LIGHT ▶ A farmer in Devon, England, damaged his iPhone by accidentally inserting it into the rear end of a cow while attempting to use it as a flashlight during calving.

HUMAN FLOWERS

▶ Take a close look at these beautiful flowers and plants—the petals and stems are made from naked human bodies! They are the work of Los Angeles, California-based artist Cecelia Webber who takes pictures of naked people and, with the help of a digital photo editing application, turns them into magical blooms. She was inspired to create the images after noticing that in a photo her own back looked like a flower petal.

AGE RESTRICTION ▶ When centenarian Marguerite Joseph from Grosse Pointe, Michigan, joined Facebook in 2011 she couldn't type in her real age. Whenever she entered her year of birth as 1908, Facebook automatically changed it to 1928, making Marguerite, who has over 1,750 followers, 20 years younger than her then 102 years of age.

RICKSHAW RACE ▶ In October 2011, 66 people from 12 countries raced from Jakarta, Indonesia, to Bangkok, Thailand, in auto rickshaws, each with a half-horsepower engine. They covered the distance of 1,864 mi (3,000 km) in two weeks.

INVISIBLE BIKE ▶ Artist and designer Joey Ruiter of Grand Rapids, Michigan, has created a street-legal motorbike that looks invisible and appears to make the rider float silently along the road. "Moto undone" has a quiet, electric engine and is encased in a shiny metal box that conceals the bike's framework. It has no speed dial or other gauges—they are all viewed through a downloadable smartphone app.

PEDAL FLIGHT ▶ A pedal-powered helicopter, the Gamera II, designed by students from the University of Maryland, successfully hovered in the air for 50 seconds in June 2012. Although it is 105 ft (32 m) wide and each of its four rotors has a span of 42 ft 7 in (13 m), the helicopter weighs just 71 lb (32.2 kg).

NEON TRUCKS ▶ Enthusiasts of Japan's Dekotora art form decorate their cargo trucks to extremes—with shiny metallics, lavish paint jobs, and so many neon lights that the rigs aren't street legal when they are turned on.

BIKER BIRD ▶ At New Hampshire Motor Speedway, Loudon, on June 17, 2012, Myles Bratter rode his motorcycle at a speed of 78 mph (125 km/h) with Rainbow, his pet Macaw parrot, perched on his shoulder, thereby setting a world speed record for riding a motorbike with an untethered bird. Bratter and Rainbow have been riding together for more than 17 years. "I raised her from an egg," he says. "The first thing she saw when she hatched was me."

▶ **IN 1975, WERNER ERHARD OF SAN FRANCISCO SENT 62,824 CHRISTMAS CARDS.** ◀

AIR MILES ▶ Ron Akana of Boulder, Colorado, spent 63 years as a flight attendant, during which time he flew an estimated 20 million mi (32 million km)—the equivalent of more than 800 trips around the world. He retired in 2012 at age 83 after completing a United Airlines flight from Denver, Colorado, to Kauai, Hawaii.

CRASH LANDING ▶ Shortly after an airplane took off from Opa-Locka Executive Airport, Florida, its door became detached in flight and crashed down onto a golf course in Broward County. Luckily, the course was closed at the time for maintenance and the plane was able to land safely at nearby Fort Lauderdale-Hollywood International Airport.

FACEBOOK WINDFALL ▶ When graffiti artist David Choe was asked to paint the office walls at Facebook's first HQ in Palo Alto, California, in 2005, he was offered payment of a few thousand dollars or the equivalent in shares. Despite thinking then that Facebook was "pointless," he took the stock and when the company was floated seven years later he stood to pocket an estimated $200 million.

GOLD CAR ▶ In 2011, Indian car manufacturer Tata created a Nano car covered in gold, silver, and jewels worth $4.6 million—the price of more than 1,500 standard model Nanos. Thirty craftsmen worked on the creation of the one-off model, using 176 lb (80 kg) of 22-carat gold, 33 lb (15 kg) of silver, and around 10,000 assorted gemstones.

TOILET BEST ▶ At a stunt show in Sydney, Australia, on May 2, 2012, stuntwoman and former motocross champion Jolene Van Vugt from Ontario, Canada, set a new land speed record for a motorized toilet of 46 mph (74 km/h). Her contraption resembles a go-kart but has a porcelain toilet in place of a driver's seat.

GHOST CAR ▶ Sci-fi fan Paul Harborne from the West Midlands, England, spent £50,000 restoring a battered 1959 Cadillac into an exact replica of Ecto-1, the *Ghostbusters* car from the 1984 movie. Available to hire, the car makes a big splash with its replica lightbars and rotating beacons.

TRUCK PILE UP

▶ *Traffic cops in Laian, China, thought they had probably seen everything until they spotted these three flatbed trucks piled on top of each other driving erratically along the highway. Having just bought the trucks, cargo firm boss Sun Lin wanted to save money on drivers and toll fees, so he asked the seller to stack them up by crane ready to be driven more than 100 mi (160 km) to his yard. He was fined $750 for his crazy idea.*

THAT'S INCREDIBLE!

YOUR UPLOADS

HUMAN VISE
▶ Ripley's were sent in this incredible submission by the strongman Pat Povilaitis ("The Human Vise") from Oak Ridge, New Jersey. Pat can stick his hand into an authentic wolf or mountain-lion trap, then lift a 275-lb (125-kg) Ford 460 engine block with the hand in the trap! The top left image proves just how strong the trap is when he tests it with fried chicken.

ROBOT HUMMINGBIRD▶ Japanese scientists are developing a robot hummingbird that will one day save lives by searching for survivors in wreckage and other areas not easily accessible to humans. The tiny, flying robot, fitted with a minute camera, flaps its wings 30 times per second—just like a real hummingbird—and researchers hope to use infrared sensors to get it to hover in midair.

FACEBOOK HUGS▶ Scientists at Massachusetts Institute of Technology have invented the Like-A-Hug—a wearable social media vest that enables people to give hugs to their friends and family on Facebook. The vest inflates whenever friends "Like" a picture, video, or status update, translating their virtual thumbs-up into a real hug.

BINOCULARS BUILDING▶ The Binoculars Building in Venice, California, one of the Google offices, gets its name from the giant pair of binoculars—45 ft (13.7 m) high and 44 ft (13.4 m) wide—that links the two disparate parts of the Frank Gehry-designed building. The entrance to the parking garage is between the lenses of the binoculars, which were created by artists Claes Oldenburg and Coosje van Bruggen.

BEE-LEAVE IT!▶ Interstate 15 in Utah was closed for several hours after a truck carrying 25 million bees overturned. Beekeepers worked overnight to recapture the insects—worth more than $100,000—which were being transported from South Dakota to California.

SADDLE SOAR▶ Felix Guirola rides a 13-ft-high (4-m) homemade, super-tall bicycle through the streets of Havana, Cuba. He pedals around at eye-level with second-story apartments, peering over pickup trucks and buses, and wears no helmet or other protective gear to break a fall.

ZOMBIES INJURED▶ Emergency medical crews called to an accident on a movie set in Toronto, Ontario, were alarmed to find the actors covered in blood and gore. They then realized that most of it was makeup because the actors were dressed as zombies for the movie *Resident Evil: Retribution*.

CRASH LANDING▶ To test the durability of iPad cases, skydivers in the United States started playing movies on iPads, then zipped them into protective cases and dropped them from a height of 1,300 ft (400 m) to see if they could survive the fall. When retrieved after their crash landing, the iPads were still playing the movies.

FIRST APPLE▶ One of the still-functioning Apple 1 computers—the first product built by Apple Computer Inc. in 1976—sold at an auction on June 15, 2012, for $374,500.

FRIED GADGETS▶ To link the consumption of gadgets and the consumption of fast food, Brooklyn, New York-based artist Henry Hargreaves photographs deep-fried iPads, MacBooks, and Game Boys. However, he doesn't cook real gadgets—instead he uses fakes made from a material called foamcore.

FREE BOAT▶ To avoid paying a $2,400 salvage fee after his 16-ft (5-m) fishing boat capsized in the Gulf of Mexico, owner Jack Roberts, from Fort Walton Beach, Florida, put the boat, plus its contents of $2,000 worth of fishing gear and $800 cash, up for sale on Craigslist for free—provided the buyer could first haul the vessel up from the seabed.

HEALTHY APP▶ An app called "SkinVision" monitors the moles on your skin for signs of skin cancer. It photographs each mole and builds a structural map, which reveals the different growth patterns of the tissues and alerts you to any abnormal development that could be an indication of melanoma.

FEEL THE PINCH

▶ Californian artist Laura Ann Jacobs has designed a bra that pinches—because it's in the shape of a crab, complete with claws. She has created dozens of wacky, brightly colored bras, incorporating everything from fish heads to fruit.

XXL JACKET ▶ Children from a school in Stockport, England, helped make a jacket that was big enough to cover more than half a tennis court. Made up of 8,832 knitted squares, the oversized jacket measured 42 x 18 ft (13 x 5.5 m).

SOUNDS FISHY ▶ Quintetto, a musical art installation by the Italian studio Quiet Ensemble, features five fish tanks that operate as five digital instruments, each playing differently depending on the position of the fish.

WEED FASHION ▶ Artist Nicole Dextras from Vancouver, Canada, has created a "Weedrobes" clothing line, with garments made from flowers, weeds, leaves, and even thorns. She began by fashioning a coat from a bunch of laurel leaves she found in an alleyway but has since branched out to design everything from a pair of shoes cut from cabbage leaves to a beautiful evening gown adorned with camellia flowers.

NO FILM ▶ Germany-based director Jay Chung once produced, wrote, and directed a 35mm movie with a crew of 20 over a period of two years—but with no film in the camera! He deliberately didn't tell the cast and crew that the nature of the project meant their efforts would never be seen.

CAMERA COSTUME ▶ When photographer Tyler Card of Grand Rapids, Michigan, needed a costume for a Halloween party, he turned himself into a fully functional Nikon camera. He made a working flash and shutter release button and attached it to his costume, which consisted of a black-painted cardboard box for the camera body and a paint bucket for the lens.

ZAPPA BUST ▶ Lithuania's capital, Vilnius, has a bronze bust of U.S. musician Frank Zappa built by members of the country's Cold War-era independence movement to celebrate his influence—even though he wasn't Lithuanian and had never even visited the country.

CONDENSED YEAR ▶ New York City-based animator Cesar Kuriyama filmed a second of his life every day for a year before editing the clips together in chronological order to create a six-minute video. His one-second snapshots, which ended with his 31st birthday in February 2012, included a marriage and a funeral.

HOLY CATASTROPHE! ▶ A scientific study of Batman's ability to fly using only his rigid cape has concluded that he would be able to glide successfully for some distance over Gotham City, but would suffer serious injuries when trying to land. Physicists at the University of Leicester, England, calculated that his cape's 15-ft-5-in (4.7-m) wingspan—about half that of a hang glider—would keep him airborne for a while, but he would be hitting the ground at 50 mph (80 km/h)—too fast to avoid possibly fatal injury.

BAGGY DRESS ▶ Over the course of three months, 16-year-old Suraya Mohd Zairin of Shah Alam, Malaysia, created a floral pattern dress from 4,000 used tea bags.

CANINE CHANNEL ▶ In February 2012, a new cable TV channel solely for dogs was launched in San Diego, California. DOGTV aims to keep dogs relaxed and entertained in the home while their owners are out at work. The sound, colors, and camera angles of the shows—most of which star animals—are all designed to have canine appeal.

SWEET MUSIC ▶ Croatian punk band Fon Biskich released a 2012 single made of chocolate. They used hard, bitter chocolate with a high-cocoa content to create a record that fans could eat when they got bored with the song.

COOKING WITH POO ▶ Saiyuud Diwong wrote a 2012 recipe book called *Cooking with Poo*, but it is not as gross as it sounds—"poo" means "crab" in Thailand and is also the chef's nickname.

UNFORGETTABLE AUDIENCE ▶ To celebrate his 50th birthday, Englishman Paul Barton dragged a piano up a mountain in Kanchanaburi Province, Thailand, to play Beethoven to blind elephants—he considered the feat a birthday present to himself. Barton, who has worked with blind elephants on the reserve for many years, sat at his piano just a few feet away from the animals.

PIE VICTIM ▶ U.S. comedian Soupy Sales (1926–2009) had an estimated 20,000 pies thrown both at himself and at the guests on his television shows in the 1950s and 1960s.

DUCT TAPE ▶ Brooke Wallace from Solomon, Kansas, made her prom dress completely out of duct tape. She used 42 rolls of duct tape to make a Western-style dress for herself and a suit for her date Mark Aylward and still had enough left over to create a purse and earrings. She spent more than 200 hours working on the outfits, hand-folding thousands of pieces of tape.

TIGHT FIT ▶ Andy Coyne of Greenville, South Carolina, wore 249 T-shirts simultaneously, the garments weighing a total of more than 200 lb (91 kg).

CORDUROY CLUB ▶ Founded by Miles Rohan, the Corduroy Appreciation Club of New York City, New York, boasts over 250 members. It meets twice a year—on January 1 and November 11 (1/1 and 11/11), on which occasions members must wear at least two items of corduroy clothing.

ICE BRA ▶ Lingerie manufacturer Triumph has created a bra containing built-in ice packs and a miniature fan to help women keep cool in summer.

THAT'S INCREDIBLE!

SUM DRESS ▶ Seventeen-year-old Kara Koskowich, who attended the Lethbridge Collegiate Institute in Alberta, Canada, made her graduation dress from her old math homework. She crafted the one-shouldered dress from 75 pieces of algebra formulae and neon Post-it® notes.

BODY PARTS ▶ London, England-based jewelry designer Percy Lau has introduced a range of pieces that looks like miniature body parts. Handcrafted in clay, the jewelry items include earrings in the shape of a human ear, finger rings in the shape of a closed mouth, and a necklace with a human nose on the end.

WRITE ON ▶ American author John Green autographed each of the 152,000 books in the first printing of his 2012 novel *The Fault in Our Stars* by signing his name for 12 hours a day, every day, for a month.

TONGUE INSURED ▶ At the height of the band's success, Kiss front man Gene Simmons had his trademark extra-long tongue insured for $1 million.

CELEBRITY TREE ▶ The daughter of Beyoncé and Jay-Z was named an honorary citizen of the Croatian town of Hvar because they named her Blue Ivy after a local tree. The celebrity couple had been impressed by the tree, which was wrapped in blue ivy, during their visit in September 2011.

SPARKLING NAILS

▶ Priced at $250,000 for a tiny bottle, Azature Black Diamond is the most expensive nail polish ever produced. Created by Los Angeles-based luxury jeweler Azature, the polish contains 267 carats of precious black diamonds and is so exclusive that only one bottle has been made.

TOILET PAPER DRESS ▶
In June 2012, Susan Brennan of Orchard Lake, Michigan, won an annual toilet-paper wedding dress contest for the second year in a row by rustling up a modern dress made out of ten rolls of toilet paper, held together with glue, packing tape, and thread, in just a week. She called her creation "Bohemian Cupcake," with the skirt part looking like layers of delicious cake frosting.

GOOD VIBRATIONS ▶ The Royal Philharmonic Orchestra played a three-hour concert in Cadogan Hall, London, England—to an audience of more than 100 plants and bulbs. The concert was to test whether musical vibrations can help stimulate plant growth.

COMEDY ORDER ▶ In addition to food and drink, customers who ordered room service at the Hotel Indigo in Edinburgh, Scotland, in April 2012 could order a 10-minute stand-up comedy routine by Janey Godley, who would come to their room and tell jokes.

BALLOONING BRIDES ▶ Thelma Levett from Leicestershire, England, made a replica of Kate Middleton's wedding dress from more than 5,000 balloons. The balloon artist, whose other balloon creations include a pink Cadillac and a bicycle, used both inflated and non-inflated balloons for the special wedding dress, which took more than four days to blow up.

DEEP VOICE ▶ The voice of U.S. singer Tim Storms can go so deep that the human ear is unable to hear it. Blessed with vocal chords twice the length of the average person's, he has a vocal range of ten octaves and can hit the note G7 (0.189Hz), the lowest note ever recorded by a human.

HAIR-RAISING

▶ Six employees and students from South Gloucestershire and Stroud College, England, created the longest hair extension in the world, an attachment stretching a hair-raising 1,185 ft (361.4 m)—that's the length of four soccer fields! The record-breaking extension, worn by Jade Bryer, took seven hours to make.

HEADBANGER

▶ Swooping to catch prey, this unlucky owl collided head-on with a pickup truck and found itself wedged in the vehicle's grill. The trucker drove 8 mi (13 km), with the owl's head still trapped in the grill, before he was able to call the Vermont Fish and Wildlife Department to rescue the bird which, incredibly, was later released unharmed.

Ouch!

GLAMOROUS GOLDFISH ▶ The world's first beauty contest for goldfish was staged in Fuzhou, China, in 2012. More than 3,000 fish from 14 different countries were lined up on rows of tables in giant bowls. There were 12 categories, including the longest and heaviest goldfish, and the fish were judged on five criteria: breed, body shape, swimming motion, color, and overall impression.

WAITING GAME ▶ A man suspected of swallowing a diamond that he had stolen from a jewelry store in Windsor, Ontario, Canada, was held in custody until it finally passed through his system—nine days later. Richard Matthews was fed fiber-rich foods to speed up the process after an X-ray also revealed the presence of a pair of artificial diamonds in his intestines.

CORPSE'S COMPANION ▶ Two years after her husband died, grieving widow Adriana Villareal of Buenos Aires, Argentina, had moved into his tomb and set up a bed, a chair, a radio, a computer with Internet access, and even a small stove next to his coffin. She visits the cemetery three times a year, spending three or four nights at a time sleeping next to her husband's embalmed corpse.

FELINE FELON ▶ A cat was caught trying to smuggle a cell phone into a Brazilian prison. Officers who spotted the cat going through the main entrance of the Judge Luiz de Oliveira Souza prison found the phone, charger, batteries, drill bits, and memory cards strapped to its body. The cat is believed to have been secretly raised by inmates and then given to visitors.

EGGLESS CHICK ▶ A hen in Welimada, Sri Lanka, gave birth to a chick without laying an egg. Instead of passing out of the hen's body and being incubated outside, the fertilized egg was incubated within the hen's reproductive system until it hatched inside her body. The chick survived but the hen died of internal wounds.

SINGING MICE ▶ A breed of mouse that lives in the mountains of Costa Rica uses song to communicate. The mice "sing" to each other their mating calls, the sounds reaching over long distances in the form of up to 20 high-pitched chirps per second.

AGORAPHOBIC OWL ▶ Gandalf, a Great Gray Owl at Knowsley Safari Park near Liverpool, England, was afraid of flying outside in the open, so his owners built a special aviary for him inside a brick shed.

GIRAFFE JOCKEY ▶ Having hand-raised Mara, a three-month-old, 6½-ft-tall (2-m), giraffe, at the Lion Park conservation area near Johannesburg, South Africa, Shandor Larenty trained her to carry him on her back. Larenty's English great uncle, Terry, worked for the famous Chipperfield's Circus in the 1950s and was the only person at the time known to be able to ride a giraffe.

MIRACLE ESCAPE ▶ Carlos Montalvo, a federal agent with the Tampa, Florida, Division of the ATF, lived to enjoy his retirement thanks to a "one-in-20-million shot" in 1987 when a drug suspect fired at him from close range, but instead of entering Montalvo's body, the bullet entered the barrel of his gun. Montalvo had moved in to make an arrest when the suspect fired from just 4 ft (1.2 m) away, but luckily both men were carrying the same kind of gun and the bullet entered the barrel of Montalvo's 9-mm Sig Sauer, where it smashed the bullet inside but spared the agent.

DUCK CALL ▶ Since 1974, the city of Stuttgart, Arkansas, has awarded a $2,000 scholarship annually to the high school senior who can make the best duck call. The scholarship honors the memories of Stuttgart's champion duck callers and duck-call makers, Chick and Sophie Major.

ROCK TV ▶ Jason Antone, who suffers from the rare genetic disorder Friedreich's ataxia, broadcasts JROCK TV, a public access television show, from his home in West Bloomfield, Michigan, and in three years has received no less than 246 calls from celebrity guests endorsing the show, including actors Chevy Chase and Josh Gad, and talk-show host Regis Philbin.

PULLED TRAIN ▶ With a harness strapped around his waist, Syrian strongman Adnan Ismail al-Awad used all his muscle power to pull a 65-ft-long (20-m) train that was full of passengers up an incline—a total weight of around 100 tons. Normally, it would take the strength of 100 horses to get the train and carriages to move.

CUCKOO CRAZY ▶ Jim and Jane Klingensmith have more than 300 cuckoo clocks in their Lake Placid, Florida, home. They began collecting the clocks in 1992 and their oldest clock dates back to the late 19th century.

WRONG NOTE ▶ Two robbers hit the wrong note when they stole a jukebox from a restaurant in San Diego, California, after mistaking it for a cash machine. The dopy duo tried to back a pick-up truck through the glass door of the restaurant, only to find that the opening was too narrow—and then they compounded their error by towing away the jukebox instead of the ATM.

REPLICA SUPERCAR ▶ Wang Jian, a mechanic and farmer from Jiangsu Province, China, built his own replica of a $1.5 million Lamborghini Reventon supercar for just $9,000. Using scrap metal, it took him over 15 months to build his dream car, but because he cannot get a license to drive it on the road, he uses it instead for transporting fertilizer!

THAT'S INCREDIBLE!

ZIP IT!

▶ These brilliant zipper lips were created by would-be makeup artists from New College, Worcestershire, England, as part of a challenge by international fashion and beauty photographer Alistair Cowin to create weird and wonderful lip designs. The students also made up lips in the design of a crab, a cat, a candy cane, a human skull, and the Stars and Stripes, and used accessories, such as pearls, black caviar, and baked beans.

PAINTED BENTLEY

British artist Paul Karslake created his artwork *Empire* by painting a Bentley Mulsanne with scenes of the British Empire.

Featuring portraits of former Prime Minister Winston Churchill and Queen Elizabeth II, as well as famous British military victories including Trafalgar and Waterloo, the car was unveiled outside the Ripley's Attraction in London, England, in June 2012 to celebrate the Queen's Diamond Jubilee.

THAT'S INCREDIBLE!

▶ Paul's Bentley sits beside the Ripley Attraction's smallest car, the Peel.

▲ Paul's portrait of Horatio Nelson, a British flag officer famous for serving in the Royal Navy during the Napoleonic Wars and the Battle of Trafalgar in 1805 when he was killed.

▲ On the top of Paul's Bentley there is a painting of a British flag on fire. He chose to paint a Bentley because it is such a British marque of car.

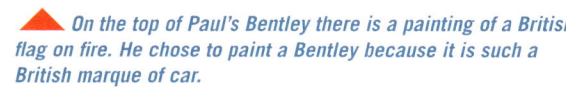

▶ It took Paul over 500 hours to complete the car.

◀ This piece depicts a scene at the Battle of Waterloo in 1815 —one of Paul's detailed artworks.

▲ The Duke of Wellington, who fought in the Battle of Waterloo (see left). The car is Paul's idea of a "potted" history of the British Empire.

31

LIGHT RELIEF ▶ Unable to compete with her neighbor's spectacular 16,000-light Christmas display, Kristina Green of Maricopa, Arizona, used a mere 900 green and red lights to spell out the word "Ditto" with an arrow pointing toward the house next door.

DEAD MAN WALKING ▶ Terrified relatives fled a funeral in Alagoinhas, Brazil, when the deceased suddenly turned up—alive. A body at the morgue had been identified as car washer Gilberto Araujo by his brother, but the first Gilberto knew about it was when he bumped into a friend in the street who told him that he was supposed to be dead and that his funeral was taking place soon. "He told me there was a coffin and that I was inside it. So I said, 'But I'm alive. Pinch me!'"

VAMPIRE HUNT ▶ When villagers near Dharmapuri, Tamil Nadu, India, thought vampires were killing their cattle in early 2012, officials offered a $2,000 cash reward to anyone who could prove conclusively that a vampire existed.

GRAVESIDE VIGIL ▶ A faithful dog has refused to leave his dead master's grave for more than six years—even though the dog was never shown the location of either the cemetery or the tomb. German shepherd Capitan ran away from home after Miguel Guzman died in 2006, but a week later the family went to the cemetery in Villa Carlos Paz, Argentina, to pay their respects and were startled to find the dog howling by the grave. Capitan sometimes goes off for a walk during the day, but at 6 p.m. sharp he lies on the grave and stays there all night.

YELLOW SUBMARINE ▶ Molly the West Highland terrier travels around the coastline of Cornwall, England, in owner Chris Garner's yellow, two-seater underwater vessel MSV Explorer to study marine life. The adventurous dog also joins him on motorcycle and quad-bike rides.

WALKING BACKWARD ▶ Hu Xianwei of Handan, China, has trained his Pekingese Zhu Zhu to walk backward on his hind legs for more than 1 mi (1.6 km) every day. The dog even glances back over his shoulder to look out for obstacles.

STOREROOM SURVIVOR ▶ Manuela the tortoise was found alive in a house in Rio de Janeiro, Brazil, despite having spent more than 30 years locked in a storeroom. She had vanished in 1982, but it was not until Leonel Almieda died in 2013 and his children began clearing out a locked second-floor junk room that they found the long-lost family pet—among a pile of broken electrical items. Animal experts believe the lucky tortoise survived all those years by nibbling termites from the wooden floor for food and licking condensation off smooth surfaces in order not to become dehydrated.

DAZZLING CEILING ▶ Each Christmas, Sylvia Pope of Swansea, Wales, decks out the ceiling of her living room with an astonishing 1,750 Christmas baubles from all over the world.

FAKE CARS ▶ Police in Wuxi City, China, have placed cardboard cutouts of squad cars by the sides of roads in a bid to slow down speeding drivers. The boards even have solar panels, which power flashing lights so that the fake cop cars look realistic at night.

LION DOG

▶ Panic spread through Norfolk, Virginia, in January 2013 after dog-owner Daniel Painter shaved the hair of his Labradoodle, Charles the Monarch, so that it looked like a lion. Worried residents called 911 to report that a big cat was roaming the streets and police officers checked with Virginia Zoo to make sure that none of its lions had escaped. Painter, who shaved his dog to look like the lion mascot of nearby Old Dominion University, said: "I tell people he's a Lab-a-lion, and half of them believe that!"

THAT'S INCREDIBLE!

SMOOCHING POOCHES▶ A "love hotel" for dogs, complete with its own fitness center, opened in 2012 in Belo Horizonte, Brazil. Dog owners pay $50 a day for their pampered pooches to have a room that comes with a heart-shaped mirror on the ceiling, red cushions on the floor, and dimmed lighting.

DRIVE-THROUGH FUNERALS▶ The Robert L. Adams funeral parlor in Los Angeles, California, offers drive-through funerals, allowing mourners to pay their last respects without having to leave the comfort of their car. The deceased is viewed through a long window made from bulletproof glass. The idea is intended to help people who have difficulty walking, as well as those with busy schedules.

HIDDEN LIGHT▶ A neon light that had been left on accidentally over 75 years ago was found behind a wall in the women's restroom during the 2012 renovation of the historic Clifton's Cafeteria in Los Angeles, California. The longest-lit neon light in the world, it had run up an estimated electric bill of $17,000 since the 1930s.

BEAR INVASION▶ Meteorologist Kurt Aaron's regular 11 p.m. weather forecast for WNEP-TV in Scranton, Pennsylvania, which is usually filmed in a landscaped outdoor area, was hastily relocated on April 23, 2012, after a mother bear and three of her cubs appeared unexpectedly on the set. Seeing the adult black bear just 10 ft (3 m) away, Aaron ran inside and did his report indoors from the studio instead.

FINGER FIGHT▶ When a suspect pointed a .38-caliber revolver at NYPD Sgt. Michael Miller, the officer managed to jam the gun by wedging his finger between the hammer and the cylinder. Although the man pulled the trigger several times, the gun would not fire and he was overpowered, leaving Sgt. Miller with nothing worse than a crushed bone in his finger tip.

DOGGIE WEDDING▶ On July 12, 2012, Baby Hope Diamond, a white Coton de Tulear rescue dog, married Chilly Pasternak, a poodle, in a wedding that cost $158,187—nearly six times the cost of the average human wedding. The doggie bride's wedding dress cost $6,000, and tickets were sold for the event to raise money for an animal charity.

MATH GENIUS▶ Using only mental calculation, India's Amit Garg solved ten math problems—each requiring him to divide ten digits by five digits—in just 5 minutes 45 seconds at Annapolis, Maryland, on March 15, 2012.

GOAT PEDICURE▶ Two people stole a tame goat from a petting zoo in San Diego, California, and returned him the next day after giving him a pedicure with pink toenails.

TATTOO RIDE

▶ Trying to keep a steady hand, Burnaby Q. Orbax tattooed his brother, Sweet Pepper Klopek, while the pair were riding on Canada's oldest and bumpiest wooden roller-coaster—at PNE Playland in Vancouver. Orbax, who had never tattooed anyone before, held the tattoo machine while the ink cap was duct-taped to Klopek's hands. The result inked on Klopek's upper right knee was a smiley face tattoo with a very long tongue.

Actually having his leg tattooed!

◀ The brothers also perform with the freak show Monsters of Schlock—Orbax has pulled a 4½-ton truck for more than 110 yd (100 m) using ropes attached to two hooks in his back, while Klopek has released 40 mousetraps on his tongue in one minute!

INDEX

Page numbers in italic refer to the illustrations

A

Aaron, Kurt (USA) 33
Ahmed, Patrice Christine (Fra) 15
airplanes
  bees delay 15
  door lands on golf course 24
  homemade 15
  long career as flight attendant 24
  runaway boy on 15
  sleeping passenger 15
Akana, Ron (USA) 24
Alam, Mohammed (USA) 15
Allen, Joel (Can) 19
Almieda, Leonel (Bra) 32
Antone, Jason (USA) 28
Araujo, Gilberto (Bra) 32
Archer, Paul (UK) 14
arm, smartphone in prosthesis 12, *12*
Armstrong, Renee (USA) 13
al-Awad, Adnan Ismail (Syr) 28
Aylward, Mark (USA) 26

B

backpacker, elderly 15
bacteria, on cell phones 13
balloons, wedding dress made of 27
bank, fraudster caught on Facebook 20
banknotes, "Money Facing" craze 13
Barton, Paul (UK) 26
Batman, landing problems 26
bears
  strongman lifts trap 25, *25*
  on weather forecast 33
beauty contest, for goldfish 28
bees
  close highway 25
  delay airplane 15
Belitsky, John (USA) 15
Beyoncé (USA) 27
bicycles
  huge 14
  quad cycle 15
  very tall 25
Bieber, Justin (Can) 18
binoculars, giant pair on building 25
birds
  agoraphobic owl 28
  owl caught in truck's grill 28, *28*
  parrot rides on motorcycle 24
  robot hummingbird 25
  songs on Twitter 22

boats
  large flotilla of 8
  nuclear-powered icebreaker 8
  shipwreck given away 25
  very fast sailing boat 15
bones, skeleton on motorcycle *10–11*, 11
books, huge number autographed 27
Bost, Russ (UK) 15
Boxall, Phil (UK) *10–11*, 11
bras
  built-in ice packs 26
  in shape of crab 26, *26*
Bratter, Myles (USA) 24
Brennan, Susan (USA) 27
bridge, train sets fire to 8, *8–9*
Brierley, Saroo (Ind) 21
Bruggen, Coosje van (Nld) 25
Bryer, Jade (UK) 27, *27*
building, giant binoculars on 25
bullet, fired into barrel of gun 28
burglar, webcam foils 20
bus driver, has heart attack 14
Butcher, Shane (USA) 21

C

camera, as fancy dress costume 26
cancer, iPhone monitors moles 25
Card, Tyler (USA) 26
cars
  cardboard squad cars to slow traffic 32
  covered in porcelain 9
  cruise-missile powered 8, *8*
  driven down subway steps 9
  driven on railway tracks 9
  driven sideways 15
  on edge of cliff 17, *17*
  Ghostbusters replica 24
  gold-covered 24
  hangs over edge of building 16, *16*
  Lamborghini built from scrap 28
  long life for 8
  mass burnout *14–15*, 15
  motorcycle made from wreckage of 9
  paintings on *30–31*, *30–31*
  powered by soda and candy 8
  racing car built from spare parts 15
  steel bars crash through windshield 16, *16*
  stolen car recovered 18
  tight parking 8
  train just avoids 17, *17*
  wood-burning stove in 14
  wrecking ball crashes into 17, *17*
Casaru, Peter (UK) 19

cats
  feeding with smartphone 18, *18*
  iPad apps for 18, *18*
  plays with iPad 19
  smuggles cell phone into prison 28
cell phones
  bacteria on 13
  cat smuggles into prison 28
  helps rescue from manhole 23
  interrupts concert 21
  monitors cancer risk 25
  more numerous than toothbrushes 19
  people dress as 21
centenarian, on Facebook 23
Cerniauskas, Tadas (Lit) 13
chair, rocker charges iPads 22
Chan, Priscilla (USA) 19
Chen, Lee Wei (UK) 19
chickens
  iPad encourages to lay 19, *19*
  lays eggless chick 28
chocolate, record made of 26
Choe, David (USA) 24
Christmas cards, sending huge number of 24
Christmas decorations 32, *32*
Chung, Jay (Ger) 26
cliff, car on edge of 17, *17*
clocks, cuckoo 29
clothes
  club wears corduroy 26
  dress made from math homework 27
  dress made of tea bags 26
  duct tape prom dress 26
  enormous jacket 26
  keyboard in jeans 19, *19*
  made from plants 26
  wearing large number of T-shirts 26
  wedding dress made of balloons 27
  wedding dress made of toilet paper 27
cola, car powered by 8
computers
  conducts wedding 12
  keyboard in jeans 19, *19*
  religious sect and 22
  very valuable 25
  very young expert 21
concert, cell phone interrupts 21
Corcoran-Fort, Liam (UK) 15
corpse, living in tomb with 28
Cowin, Alistair (UK) 29, *29*
cows
  iPhone in rear end of 23
  massive 21, *21*
Coyne, Andy (USA) 26
crab, bra in shape of 26, *26*

D

death, Facebook postings after 20
Defrees, Brian (USA) 13
Dextras, Nicole (Can) 26
diamonds
  in nail polish 27, *27*
  thief swallows 28
Dickson, Sofya and Peter (UK) 22
Diwong, Saiyuud (Tha) 26
dogs
  balancing act 18
  feeding with smartphone 18, *18*
  hotel for 33
  looks like lion 32, *32*
  refuses to leave master's grave 32
  in submarine 32
  television channel for 26
  walks backward on hind legs 32
  wedding for 33
Donghi, Father Massimo (Ita) 18
donkeys, Wi-Fi routers on 13
door, child climbs 22
Druais, Anne (Aus) 19
duck callers, scholarships for 28
duct tape, prom dress made of 26
Duke of Wellington (UK) 31, *31*

E

eBay
  Homer Simpson-like blob of glue sold on 13
  man sells old life on 21
  sale of potions banned 13
elephants, piano played to 26
Elizabeth II, Queen
  flotilla of boats 8
  "Money Facing" craze 13
  portrait on car 30, *30*
Elliott, Patrick and Linda (UK) 15
Ellison, Johno (UK) 14
Erhard, Werner (USA) 24
Excel spreadsheets, young champion 19

F

face, blasted with jet of air 13
Facebook
  bank robber caught on 20
  centenarian on 23
  hugs on 25
  judge's profile 22
  long card game on 18
  "Money Facing" craze 13
  popular taxidermy site 13
  postings after death 20
  record number of comments on 20
  record status update 19
  saves paralyzed man 19

Farhan-Roopkotha, Wasik (Ban) 21
fingers, portraits on 18, *18*
fish
    beauty contest for goldfish 28
    large fish on motorcycle 9, *9*
    piranha used as scissors 20
    play music 26
flowers, human bodies as *22–23*, 23
flying
    flying suits 9
    landing problems for Batman 26
flying saucer, homemade 15
funerals
    drive-through 33
    for wrong man 32

G
Garg, Amit (Ind) 33
Garner, Chris (UK) 32
Gehry, Frank (USA) 23
ghost, photograph of 20, *20*
giraffe, riding 28
Gith, Philip (Aus) 21
goat, pedicure for 33
Godley, Janey (UK) 27
gold-covered car 24
goldfish, beauty contest for 28
Google Earth, mother traced via 21
Google Street View, bizarre images on 21, *21*
graffiti, artist makes fortune 24
Grant, Terry (UK) 15
grave, dog refuses to leave master's 32
Green, John (USA) 27
Green, Kristina (USA) 32, *32*
Grobe, Fritz (USA) 8
Guirola, Felix (Cub) 25
guns
    bullet fired into barrel of 28
    delivered instead of TV 12
    jammed with finger 33
Guzman, Miguel (Arg) 32

H
Habay, Alex (USA) 17, *17*
hair extensions, very long 27, *27*
Han Yue (Chn) 8
hands
    give manhole warning 14, *14*
    portraits on fingers 18, *18*
Hanson, Miguel (USA) 12
Harborne, Paul (UK) 24
Hargreaves, Henry (USA) 25
hearse, stretch 15
helicopter, pedal-powered 24
Henkel, Kathleen (USA) 18
Herbert, Christopher (UK) 13

Herrera, Carlos (USA) 18, *18*
Hodgson, Tracey (UK) 20
Horvitz, Seth (USA) 12
hotels
    comedy routine for guests 27
    for dogs 33
Howell, Charlotte (UK) 20, *20*
Hu Xianwei (Chn) 32
hugs, on Facebook 25

I
ice packs, in bras 26
Internet
    Angry Brides game 20
    marriage role-playing game 20
    "milking" craze 12, *12*
    "Money Facing" craze 13
    sneaker hoax 13, *13*
    tattoos of addresses 20, *20*
    webcam foils burglar 20
    Wi-Fi routers on donkeys 13
iPads
    apps for cats 18, *18*
    cat plays with 19
    deep-fried 25
    dropped from height 25
    encourages chicken to lay 19, *19*
    orangutans use 20
    rocking chair charges 22
    watching wedding on 13
iPhones
    monitors moles 25
    in prosthetic arm 12, *12*
    in rear end of cow 23

J
jacket, enormous 26
Jacobs, Laura Ann (USA) 26, *26*
Jay-Z (USA) 27
jeans, keyboard in 19, *19*
jellyfish, swimming with 6, *6–7*
jewelry, miniature body parts 27
Joel, Billy (USA) 20
Johnson, Nick (UK) 18
Joseph, Marguerite (USA) 23
jukebox, stolen 28

K
Karslake, Paul (UK) 30–31, *30–31*
Kerekes, Ashley (USA) 13
Klingensmith, Jim and Jane (USA) 28
Klopek, Sweet Pepper (Can) 33, *33*
Kmit, Lukas (Svk) 21
Koskowich, Kara (Can) 27
Kuriyama, Cesar (USA) 26
Kurobasa, Domagoj (Cro) 22

L
Lady Gaga (USA) 18
Langeder, Hannes (Aut) 15
Larenty, Shandor (SA) 28
Lau, Percy (UK) 27
Lee Su (Chn) 19
Leray, Emile (Fra) 9
Levett, Thelma (UK) 27
light, left on for long time 33
lion, dog looks like 32, *32*
lips, make-up competition 29, *29*
lizard, "eats" on-screen insects 21

M
McDonald, Jeremiah (USA) 18
McFarlane, Juliet (UK) 19
Maier, Boris (Swi) 15
Major, Chick and Sophie (Ger) 28
manholes
    cell phone helps rescue from 23
    warning hand 14, *14*
map, of wrong place 19
marching band, recreates video game images 22
math
    dress made from homework 27
    solving problems at speed 33
Matthews, Cathy (USA) 20
Matthews, Richard (Can) 28
mice, singing 28
Middleton, Kate (UK) 27
"milking" craze 12, *12*
Miller, Michael (USA) 33
"Money Facing" craze 13
Montalvo, Carlos (USA) 28
Morris, Tom (UK) 12, *12*
motorcycles
    fallen rider sets off speed camera 15
    homemade 15
    invisible 24
    large fish on 9, *9*
    made from wreckage of car 9
    parrot on rider's shoulder 24
    skeleton on *10-11*, 11
    snake hides in 11, *11*, 20
mountain, piano dragged up 26
movies
    filming life 26
    no film in camera 26
music
    cell phone interrupts concert 21
    fish play 26
    musician celebrated in unvisited country 26
    plants listen to 27
    young pianist 20

N
nail polish, diamonds in 27, *27*
Nelson, Horatio (UK) 31, *31*
New York City, subway system 9
Nijs, Erik de (Nld) 19, *19*

O
Oddie, Bill (UK) 22
Oldenburg, Claes (USA) 25
orangutans, use iPads 20
Orbax, Burnaby Q. (Can) 33, *33*

P
Painter, Daniel (UK) 32, *32*
paintings, on car 30–31, *30–31*
paralyzed man, Facebook saves 19
pedicure, for goat 33
photograph, of ghost 20, *20*
pianos
    dragged up mountain 26
    young pianist 20
pies, thrown at comedian 26
piranha, used as scissors 20
plants
    clothes made from 26
    listen to music 27
police, cardboard cars to slow traffic 32
Pope, Sylvia (UK) 32
porcelain, car covered in 9
Povilaitis, Pat (USA) 25, *25*
Prideaux, Trevor 12, *12*
priest, on cruise ship 18
prison, cat smuggles cell phone into 28
Prokop, Pascal (Swi) 14
Purnell, Leigh (UK) 14

R
recipe book, unusual title 26
record, made of chocolate 26
Rich, Laura (USA) 18
rickshaws
    auto rickshaw race 24
    poop-powered 9
Rickwood, Rebecca (UK) 19
road, bees close 25
robberies
    fraudster caught on Facebook 20
    jukebox stolen 28
    thief swallows diamond 28
    webcam foils burglar 20
Roberts, Jack (USA) 25
robot hummingbird 25
Rohan, Miles (USA) 26
roller-coaster, tattooing on 33, *33*
Rossy, Yves (Swi) 9
Ruiter, Joey (USA) 24
Russell, Bob (USA) 18

S

Safe, Laura (UK) 22
Sales, Soupy (USA) 26
Shan Dan (Chn) 16, *16*
shipwreck, given away 25
shoes, Internet hoax 13, *13*
Shu Mansheng (Chn) 15
Simmons, Gene (USA) 27
skydiving, video glasses 20
Smit, Tim (Nld) 19, *19*
snakes, hide in motorcycle 11, *11*, 20
soccer, tweeting record broken 13
Sopo, Maxi (USA) 20
Speight, Rebekah (USA) 21
Stender, Paul (USA) 8, *8*
Storms, Tim (USA) 27
submarine, dog in 32
subways
  car driven down steps 9
  New York City 9
Sun Lin (Chn) 24, *24*

T

T-shirts, wearing large number of 26
tattoos
  Internet addresses 20, *20*
  on roller-coaster 33, *33*
taxidermy, popular Facebook site 13
taxis, long journeys in 15
tea bags, dress made of 26
telephones
  bacteria on cell phones 13
  cat smuggles into prison 28
  cell phone interrupts concert 21
  cell phones more numerous than toothbrushes 19
  feeding pets with smartphone 18, *18*
  helps rescue from manhole 23
  monitors cancer risk 25
  people dress as 21
  smartphone in prosthetic arm 12, *12*
television
  broadcast from home 28
  channel for dogs 26
  newsreader makes news 22
Thébault, Alain (Fra) 15
toilet, motorized 24
toilet paper, wedding dress made of 27
tomb, living in 28
tongue, insured 27
toothbrushes, cell phones more numerous 19
Torres, Fernando (Spa) 13
tortoise, survives in storeroom 32
trains
  car driven on tracks 9
  discouraging passengers on roof 9
  ghost trains 8
  just avoids car 17, *17*
  sets fire to bridge 8, *8–9*
  strongman pulls 28
tree, baby named after 27
tree house, built of recycled materials 19
trucks
  highly decorated 24
  owl caught in grill 28, *28*
  stack of 24, *24*
Twitter 18, 21
  bird songs on 22
  mistaken identities on 13, 20
  tweeting record broken 13

V

Vaillancourt, Patrick (Can) 20
vampires, reward for proof of 32
van, road barrier pierces *16–17*, 17
Van Vugt, Jolene (Can) 24
Veitch, Rachel (USA) 8
video games
  banned in Iran 13
  controls washing machine 19
  dressing as characters from 12
  long game on Facebook 18
  marching band recreates images 22
Villareal, Adriana (Arg) 28
voice, very deep 27
Voltz, Stephen (USA) 8
Von Tease, Dito (Ita) 18, *18*
Vu Tung Lam (Vnm) 15

W

Wallace, Brooke (USA) 26
Walmark, Ethan (USA) 20
Wang Jian (Chn) 28
washing machine, video game controls 19
Webber, Cecelia (USA) *22–23*, 23
webcam foils burglar 20
wedding dresses
  made of balloons 27
  made of toilet paper 27
weddings
  Angry Brides game 20
  computer conducts 12
  for dogs 33
  Facebook likes 19
  Internet role-playing game 20
  invaded by computer game fans 19
  watching on iPad 13
weights, strongman pulls train 28
Wesley, Diana (USA) 12
Westerman, Natalie (UK) 20
Wilborn, Jamie (USA) 13
wingsuits 9
Wood, Ashley (UK) 19, *19*
Wright, Keith (Aus) 15
Wuebben, Dan (USA) 15
Wuitschick, Jeremy (USA) 14

Y

Yang Junsheng (Chn) 16, *16*
YouTube
  interview with 12-year-old self 18
  "milking" craze 12, *12*
  piranha used as scissors 20
  snake on motorcycle 20
  time-lapse video of trip on 13
  young pianist 20

Z

Zairin, Suraya Mohd (Mal) 26
Zappa, Frank (USA) 26
Zhang Lianzhi (Chn) 9
Zhang Yali (Chn) 14
zombies, medical crew called to 25
Zuckerberg, Mark (USA) 19

ACKNOWLEDGMENTS

Cover (l) Caters News; **4** Caters News; **6–7** Caters News; **8** (t) Caters News, (b) Western Times; **9** (b) Western Times, (t) AA/ABACA/Press Association Images; **10–11** M & Y Agency Ltd/Rex Features; **11** (b) Rex Features; **12** (t) Caters News, (b) SWNS.com; **13** Rayfish.com; **14** (t) Quirky China News/Rex Features; **14–15** (b) AAP/Press Association Images; **16** Quirky China News/Rex Features; **17** (c) Ross Parry Agency, (b) Network Rail/Rex Features, (t) Tim Hahn/AP/Press Association Images; **18** (l) Pintofeed, (t) Gianluca Regnicoli; **19** (t) SWNS, (b) Caters News; **20** (t) Charlotte Howell, (b) Benoit Aquin/Polaris/eyevine; **21** (t) KPA/Zuma/Rex Features, (b) Cathy Coppini; **22–23** Cecelia Webber, www.ceceliawebber.com; **24** Europics; **25** (c/l) Luke Kelly, (c/r, b) Ryan Ganley; **26** Barcroft Media via Getty Images; **27** (t) WENN.com, (b) TheSkillsShow.com/WENN; **28** Vermont Fish & Wildlife Department; **29** Alistair Cowin/Rex Features; **32** (t) Ross D. Franklin/AP/Press Association Images, (b) Stephen M. Katz/AP/Press Association Images; **33** Syx Langemann; **Back cover** Cathy Coppini

Key: t = top, b = bottom, c = center, l = left, r = right, sp = single page, dp = double page

All other photos are from Ripley Entertainment Inc.
Every attempt has been made to acknowledge correctly and contact copyright holders and we apologize in advance for any unintentional errors or omissions, which will be corrected in future editions.